Amelia Bedelia

Means Business

#1

Amelia Bedelia
Means Business

by Herman Parish

pictures by Lynne Avril

me

Greenwillow Books
An Imprint of HarperCollins Publishers

Gouache and black pencil were used to prepare the black-and-white art.

Amelia Bedelia is a registered trademark of Peppermint Partners, LLC.

Amelia Bedelia Means Business. Text copyright © 2013 by Herman S. Parish III. Illustrations copyright © 2013 by Lynne Avril. All rights reserved. No part of this book may be used or reproduced in any manner whatsoever without written permission except in the case of brief quotations embodied in critical articles and reviews. Printed in the United States of America. For information address HarperCollins Children's Books, a division of HarperCollins Publishers, 10 East 53rd Street, New York, NY 10022. www.harpercollinschildrens.com

Library of Congress Cataloging-in-Publication Data

Parish, Herman.

Amelia Bedelia means business / by Herman Parish ; illustrated in black-and-white by Lynne Avril.

p. cm.

"Greenwillow Books."

Summary: "Young Amelia Bedelia will do almost anything for a shiny new bicycle. Her parents say they'll split the cost with her, and that means Amelia Bedelia needs to put the pedal to the metal and earn some dough! With Amelia Bedelia anything can happen, and it usually does."—Provided by publisher.

ISBN 978-0-06-209497-1 (hardback)—ISBN 978-0-06-209496-4 (pbk. ed.)

ISBN 978-0-06-227054-2 (pob)

[1. Moneymaking projects—Fiction. 2. Humorous stories.] I. Avril, Lynne, (date) ill. II. Title.

PZ7.P2185Apm 2013 [Fic]—dc23 2012024392

13 14 15 16 17 CG/RRDH 10 9 8 7 6 5 4 3

 Greenwillow Books

Paul Otto means business, too!—H. P.

For Jeffery and Paris—L. A.

Contents

Chapter 1

Money Is the Route

Amelia Bedelia never meant to lead a pack of dogs on a wild-goose chase. She never meant to steal something and then sell it. She never meant to make someone look bad (very bad) or lead a parade astray or even stomp on a piece of perfectly delicious cherry pie. But all that and more actually happened.

Amelia Bedelia needed to earn some money. The truth was, Amelia Bedelia needed to earn a *lot* of money. Maybe that was the real problem. Earning *some* money would have been easy.

Amelia Bedelia could have planted petunias for a neighbor or fed a cat while its owner was on vacation. But such small jobs would never have earned the wheelbarrows full of money Amelia Bedelia needed to make.

It all started innocently enough when Amelia Bedelia decided that she wanted a new bike. But then one thing led to another until the mayor of Amelia Bedelia's town finally said, "That Amelia Bedelia—she means business!" Here's what happened. . . .

Chapter 2

T.H.E. Bike

Amelia Bedelia adored her bike. It was a great bike. It was fast and dependable and she had learned to ride on it. She could tell you how it had gotten every dent. She could tell you what had chipped each fragment of paint from the frame and what had made those rusty scratches on the chrome. She could match each insult

to her bike to an injury on her
body: scabs on her knees, scrapes
to her elbows, bruises on her shins,
and a tiny sliver of a scar under her chin.

Amelia Bedelia had parked her bike at
the bike rack. She was about to go into
school when she saw some kids buzzing
around Suzanne Scroggins.

Suzanne was a new girl this year. She
told all her friends to call her Suzi. Amelia
Bedelia still called her Suzanne,
even though Amelia Bedelia
sat right behind her.
Amelia Bedelia had
never figured out
why Suzanne was
so crabby and bossy

every day. Every day except for today, of course, since it was the last day of school before vacation.

Amelia Bedelia noticed the difference right away. Suzanne was smiling from ear to ear! Then Amelia Bedelia saw why. Suzanne had a new bike. It was THE MOST BEAUTIFUL BIKE IN THE WORLD. Amelia Bedelia was speechless, but she did make a sound. It was the takes-your-breath-away inhaling sound that you can't control when you see something amazing.

T.H.E. BIKE was painted a rich emerald green, with metal flakes that sparkled like diamonds floating just beneath the smooth enamel surface. Gleaming chrome reflected the morning sun, dazzling Amelia Bedelia's eyes. She tried to look away, but she could not take her eyes off the bike. It hurt to look. It hurt more not to look.

Every inch of the bike was so streamlined that it looked as though it was still moving, even after Suzanne had parked it.

From the back of her throat, Amelia Bedelia managed to croak, "Nice bike."

"Thank you," said Suzanne. "But bikes are bikes."

"That's true," said Amelia Bedelia. "Just two wheels with spokes."

"And lots of gears," said Suzanne.

"I don't have any gears," said Amelia Bedelia.

"Two tires, definitely," said Suzanne.

"Not really," said Amelia Bedelia. "I don't get too tired without gears."

"Brakes?" said Suzanne.

"Sometimes my bike breaks," said Amelia Bedelia. "Then my dad fixes it."

The bell rang. It was time to go inside. As Suzanne locked her bike at the rack, she said, "Don't forget to lock up your bike, Amelia Bedelia." That's when the truth hit Amelia Bedelia. She had never locked up her bike. She didn't have to, because it wasn't worth stealing. Who would want it, after seeing T.H.E. BIKE? Amelia Bedelia didn't, that's for sure.

Everyone followed Suzanne into school, leaving Amelia Bedelia to ponder the

difference between the two bikes. She felt bad for her bike. She felt bad about feeling bad about her bike. She felt bad, period. Finding out that life is unfair was no way to start the day, and it was certainly no way to start school vacation.

That afternoon after school, Amelia Bedelia avoided everyone, even her friends. She hid behind the Dumpster, listening to the laughter and the jokes and the cries of "Have a good break!" Finally Amelia Bedelia got on her bike and rode home. She took the back way so no one would see her.

Chapter 3

There but for the Grace . . .

". . . And please," said Amelia Bedelia, "bring me a new bike. Amen."

After she finished saying grace, Amelia Bedelia dove into her supper. Her parents did not begin to eat. They just looked at her, then at each other.

Her mom arched

an eyebrow as high as it would go. Her dad opened his eyes super wide for a couple of seconds, as if someone had stepped on his stomach.

Had Amelia Bedelia been paying attention instead of twirling her spaghetti and dreaming about bikes, she would have seen this secret "eye talk" that all parents use to communicate with each other when their kids are present.

Amelia Bedelia's father unfolded his napkin, spread it on his lap, and then asked, "So, has anyone seen any nice bikes lately?"

Amelia Bedelia sat up straight, without having to be told, and exclaimed, "You wouldn't believe the bike I saw today!"

She spent the next ten minutes giving her parents an inch-by-inch description of THE MOST BEAUTIFUL BIKE IN THE WORLD, down to the last spoke.

"Goodness," said Amelia Bedelia's mother. "A bike that special must cost an arm and a leg."

Amelia Bedelia shook her head. "I would never pay that much," she said. "You need both your arms to steer a bike like that, and both legs to pedal it."

"That's a good point," said her father. "You certainly need to be big and strong to ride a bike like that."

"Yes," said her mother. "So take a bite of your broccoli before it gets cold."

Amelia Bedelia took an extra-large bite.

"How far away is Christmas?" she asked.

"A long way away," said her mother.

Amelia Bedelia took a much smaller bite of her broccoli. "How far away is my birthday?"

"Even farther," said her father.

"Did I get all of my allowance this week?"

"Every penny," said her father. "But remember, you'll have to pay *me* if you talk with your mouth full."

Amelia Bedelia closed her mouth. She chewed and chewed. Then she swallowed and said, "Could I get an early Christmas present and an early birthday present? A new bike is the only thing you'd have to give me, ever, for years and years."

"Well," said her mother, "I think it would be better if a bike wasn't just *given* to you."

Amelia Bedelia looked down at her plate. Her stomach hurt. Now she wished

she had not eaten any broccoli at all. Since she was looking at her plate, she once again missed the eye talk between her parents. This time, her mom's eyes grew wider while both of her dad's eyebrows arched high enough to graze the ceiling.

"I agree," said her dad. "You should work for a new bike and earn the money for at least half of it."

Amelia Bedelia smiled and looked at her parents. "Which half costs more?" she said. "The front half or the back half?"

"They don't sell bikes that way, honey," said her mother.

Then her father said, "I'll tell you what . . ."

what??   "What?" asked Amelia Bedelia. "What about what? What do you have to tell me about 'what'? Can we please keep talking about my bike instead of 'what'?"

Amelia Bedelia's father patiently refilled his water glass. "We can't afford to buy a fancy bike like that," he said. "But I can meet you halfway."

Amelia Bedelia slid off her chair. She walked exactly halfway around the table and stood there. Her mom and dad stared at each other, then back at her.

"Okay," said Amelia Bedelia.

½ WAY

18

"Here I am. Are you going to meet me halfway or not?"

Amelia Bedelia's dad stood up and walked halfway around the table to meet her. He said, "We will pay for half the cost of a new bike, but you will have to pay for the other half."

He held out his right hand. Amelia Bedelia looked at it.

"I can't pay you my half tonight," she said.

"Of course not," said her father. "Tonight we'll make an agreement. In business, when you agree to do something, you shake the other person's hand." .

Amelia Bedelia grabbed his wrist and

shook his hand as hard as she could, up
and down, up and—

"Owwwie!" said her father.

"Not like that, sweetie," said her
mother. "This is how you shake hands."
Her mother showed her how to shake
hands with her father.

"Make it a firm handshake," she said. "Your hand shouldn't feel like a dead fish or a wet noodle." Then her parents gave each other a hug.

"You should probably leave out the hug part, sweetie," said her mother.

"Why?" asked Amelia Bedelia. "I love Dad."

She shook her father's hand and then her mother's hand. Then Amelia Bedelia hugged both of them together.

"Family hug!" she hollered.

When they were all hugged out, Amelia Bedelia's father said, "Now, Amelia Bedelia, let's have dessert and talk about how you're going to earn your half of that bike."

Chapter 4

"You're Hired!"

Since the next day was Saturday, Amelia Bedelia and her parents did what they always did on Saturdays. After Amelia Bedelia's swimming lesson, they had lunch at Pete's Diner.

Pete's was mobbed. They had to sit at the counter instead of their favorite booth. Amelia Bedelia loved sitting at the counter. She loved being close to the action, hearing the orders called out, watching them get filled, and seeing everyone working together to make the diner run smoothly.

While they waited for their food, Amelia Bedelia asked her parents what kinds of jobs they had when they were growing up.

"I did all sorts of odd jobs," said her dad.

"My job doesn't have to be odd," said Amelia Bedelia. "I don't have to be a lion tamer or something unusual. It can be a normal, regular job, so long as it pays me a lot."

"When I was young," said her mother,

"I worked as a waitress.
I made buckets of
money. My
customers
always gave me big tips."

"That sounds
kinda fun," said Amelia Bedelia. "Did they
ever tip you so much that you fell over?"

Before her mother could answer, the
food arrived. Their usual waitress was so
busy that the owner of the diner, Pete,
served them.

"Sorry, folks," he said as he put down
their plates. "I am very
shorthanded today."
Amelia Bedelia looked
closely at his hands.

They looked like they were the regular length. Not too short, not too long. Then she looked at the french fries in front of her.

"Yum!" she said, and she gave the ketchup bottle an extra-hard squeeze. The ketchup SQUIIIRRRRRRRRRTed right over the top of the fries and onto Pete's clean white apron.

"Hey!" shouted Pete. "Look out! Ketchup on the loose!"

Amelia Bedelia thought she was in trouble . . . until Pete chuckled and asked, "Do I look like a french fry to you?"

"No," said Amelia Bedelia. "But you do look like you need some help. Do you have a job for me?"

Pete looked at Amelia Bedelia's parents.

They both smiled and shrugged.

"We come here every Saturday," said her father. "She knows your routine."

Her mother added, "She's a good worker. Amelia Bedelia will do exactly what you tell her to do. And she's on vacation now, so she has spare time."

Pete leaned forward to take a good look at Amelia Bedelia. "I wonder," he said. "Can you cut the mustard?"

"I've never tried that," said Amelia Bedelia. "But I sure can squirt the ketchup."

Pete laughed. "You sure can! Okay, I'll give it a try. You're hired. You can be an official Pete's Diner waitress in training."

Amelia Bedelia reached out and gave Pete a firm handshake. Was that his short hand, she wondered? Honestly, she felt like hugging him, too. Instead, she hugged her parents.

"Congratulations, sweetie!" said her mom.

"That's my girl!" said her dad. "You landed your very first job."

"You're hired!" Those were magic words to Amelia Bedelia. Those words meant that her dream bike would soon be a reality. She gobbled down her fries, said good-bye to her parents, then slid off her

stool and skipped into the kitchen. Doris, their regular waitress, found her a uniform.

"This is the smallest size we've got, honey," Doris said.

Doris slipped the uniform over Amelia Bedelia's clothes. She tucked here and folded there. Finally, after half a dozen safety pins had been pinned and a bunch

of twisty ties had been twisted and tied, Amelia Bedelia was ready for action. "You look nervous," said Doris. "Don't worry, I'll show you the ropes. Follow me!"

How cool, thought Amelia Bedelia. What kind of ropes would Doris show her? Cowboy lassos? Mountain climbing ropes? Those thick lines that tie ships up to the pier? Maybe this would turn out to be an odd job, after all.

"Well, well," said Pete when Amelia Bedelia and Doris came out of the kitchen. "Look at you!"

"I can't," said Amelia Bedelia. "There's no mirror."

"Well, believe me," he said. "You look like a real waitress. Now, I have only one rule. Can you read that?" He pointed at a sign over the cash register.

Amelia Bedelia read the sign out loud: "The customer is *always* right!" Someone (probably Pete) had underlined the word "always" in red.

"Just remember that the customer is always right," said Pete, "and you'll never go wrong around here."

Wrong? thought Amelia Bedelia. What could possibly go wrong?

Chapter 5

When Right Was Wrong

Amelia Bedelia went right to work. She did all the little things that Doris usually did but didn't have time to do on such a busy day. Amelia Bedelia refilled ketchup bottles, poured more salt and pepper into the shakers, folded napkins, and got more sugar and sweetener packets. Most of all, she had fun.

Then the unthinkable happened. Suzanne and three girls from Amelia Bedelia's class walked through the door. Amelia Bedelia sank down behind the counter like the *Titanic*. What should she do? She was excited to tell them about her new job, but she also felt super embarrassed in her waitress uniform.

Amelia Bedelia inched up to take a peek. The girls had chosen a booth where they couldn't see her. Whew! Now if she just stayed out of sight . . . stayed quiet . . .

"Amelia Bedelia!"

"Eeee-*ahhh!*" Amelia Bedelia nearly jumped out of her skin. Luckily, it was only Doris.

"Calm down, honey," Doris said.

33

"Your mom was right. You *are* a good worker. Here's a treat—you deserve it!"

She handed Amelia Bedelia a strawberry milkshake in a tall, frosty glass.

"Thanks, Doris!" said Amelia Bedelia.

As she took her first sip, a big man walked in and sat down at the counter.

He was wearing a bright orange baseball cap and a patch on his  shirt that said MIKE. Amelia Bedelia offered him a menu.

"No, thanks," he said. "I know what I want."

"Good," said Doris. "That's as easy as pie."

"And I'm in a big hurry,"

he added. "My truck's still running."

"No problem," said Doris. "At Pete's Diner, fast service is a piece of cake."

"I'm sure glad to hear that," he said. "Please bring me a big piece of cherry pie."

Doris turned to Amelia Bedelia and said, "This is a simple one. You can fill his order while I go talk to the cook. I'll be back in a few."

Amelia Bedelia smiled and nodded to the man. Then she went to the dessert case.

As she stood there gazing at all of the yummy desserts, she realized that she had completely forgotten what the man had ordered. She turned her brain inside out. Was it "easy as pie" or was it "a piece of cake"? Was it easier to bake a pie than a cake? You don't have to frost a pie, that's easier. But you don't have to roll out dough for a cake. Then again . . .

"Hello, there," Mike called. "Did you forget me? I'm really in a hurry!"

Fast, said Amelia Bedelia to herself. *That's a piece of cake. That's it!*

She brought him a piece of cake.

"Cake?" he said. "I ordered pie!"

"Sorry," said Amelia Bedelia. "I'm just learning."

"I can tell," said Mike. "And I'm late. Just bring me a piece of cherry pie—and step on it!"

Amelia Bedelia dashed off to get his pie. But now she was more confused than ever. Why did he want her to step on it?

She remembered Pete's rule. The customer is *always* right! She dashed back to Mike and put his pie on the counter.

"At last," he said, sighing happily. As he lifted his fork to take the first bite, Amelia Bedelia climbed up onto the counter.

"What are you doing?" asked Mike. "Hey! Hey! Get off the counter!"

Just then, Pete came out of the kitchen. "What's all the commotion?" he asked. "Amelia Bedelia, what are you—"

Amelia Bedelia raised
her foot and stepped on that
tasty slice of pie with all her might. Gooey
cherry pie filling spurted all over the
counter, all over Mike, and all over Pete.

Mike leaped to his feet. "That does it!"
he yelled. "I'm out of here!"

"Wait!" Pete called. He got an entire

cherry pie from the dessert case and raced out to the parking lot after him.

By the time Pete came back in, Doris had returned, and she and Amelia Bedelia had wiped off the counter. Amelia Bedelia felt awful. It didn't help that she could hear giggles from a certain booth. She'd recognize Suzanne's laugh anywhere.

"I'm sorry about the mess on your apron," Amelia Bedelia said to Pete.

Pete looked at his apron. Then he said, "At least it matches that ketchup stain."

Doris laughed. Amelia Bedelia smiled.

Pete sighed and shook his head. "I don't know what to say, Amelia Bedelia, except that I have to let you go."

"Go where?" asked Amelia Bedelia.

"Go home," said Pete. "I'm sorry."

"I am sorry, too," said Amelia Bedelia.
"I wanted to see those ropes and cut some
mustard. And I really wanted a big tip."

"I've got a tip for you," said Pete. "You
should get an office job. I don't think the
world is ready for you to be a waitress."

Doris helped Amelia Bedelia out of her
uniform. Then she slipped five dollars into
her pocket. "Here, honey," she said. "You
were the best
waitress in training
I've ever had."

Then Amelia
Bedelia left and
began the *lonnnnnng*
walk home.

Chapter 6

"You're Fired!"

Amelia Bedelia was glad she had to walk through the park to get home. Walking by the trees and flowers helped her think. What was she going to tell her mom and dad? Her very first job had lasted less than an hour. They might not feel so proud of her now.

Amelia Bedelia spied a big bed of flowers. *I know,* she said to herself, *I'll bring Mom some flowers. Then she won't be mad at me.* Amelia Bedelia had seen that work for her father when her mom was upset with him. It was worth a try now.

She picked a bunch of flowers in different colors and surrounded them with a circle of daisies. Daisies were her mom's favorite (hers, too). She had just finished making the bouquet when a policeman walked up.

"Little girl," he said. "Where did you get all those flowers?"

"Right there," said Amelia Bedelia. "I didn't leave many, but there are still enough for you."

The policeman looked where she pointed. "You've cleaned out that entire flower bed!" he said.

"No, I didn't," said Amelia Bedelia. "It's still very dirty."

The policeman shook his head. "You can't pick flowers in the park. They're for everyone who lives here to enjoy!"

"I live here," said Amelia Bedelia. "So does my mom. I picked these for her."

"You can't do that," the policeman said. "In fact, you shouldn't even be standing here. Can you read that?" He pointed at a sign stuck in the lawn.

"It says 'Keep off the grass,'" said Amelia Bedelia.

"That means you," said the policeman.

Amelia Bedelia looked at her feet. Then she looked at the policeman's feet.

"What about you?" she asked. "You're standing on the grass, too."

The policeman looked annoyed. "Are you talking back to me?" he asked sternly.

Amelia Bedelia wasn't sure what to do. She wanted to answer him, but she'd have to talk back to do it.

Finally she said, "Yes. But you started talking to me first. So I talked back to you, then you talked back to me and I talked back to you, so you—"

The policeman blew his whistle.

"Enough!" he said. "I'll let you off with a warning this time. Now take those flowers home to your mother."

"I promise I will," said Amelia Bedelia, as she waved good-bye. "Thanks!"

Amelia Bedelia walked slowly down the path. As soon as the policeman was out of sight, she sat down on a park bench to rest for a minute.

A woman was sitting at the other end of the bench with her dog. She didn't look very happy. In fact, she looked very sad.

"What lovely flowers," she said to Amelia Bedelia.

"I'd like to give them to you," said Amelia Bedelia, "to cheer you up. But I just promised to take them to my mom."

"How sweet of you," said the woman. Then she blew her nose. "Sorry if I look upset. My boss just gave me a pink slip."

"Sounds pretty," said Amelia Bedelia.

"Pretty?" she said. "It wasn't pretty at all!"

"That's too bad," said Amelia Bedelia.

"Maybe pink isn't your color. My mom likes white slips with lacy stuff on the top."

A curious look came over the woman's face. Then she burst out laughing and kept on laughing until tears streamed down her cheeks.

"Thank you," she said. "I needed a good laugh today. My name is Diana. What's yours?"

"I'm Amelia Bedelia."

"Meet Buster," said Diana. Her dog held up its paw for Amelia Bedelia to shake.

"Wow," Amelia Bedelia said. "Buster has a firm paw shake."

"Buster is the best," said Diana. "He

doesn't care that I was just let go from my job."

"Me, too!" said Amelia Bedelia. Then she told Diana what had happened at Pete's Diner. Diana laughed even harder when she heard about stepping on the pie.

"We've got a lot in common," said Diana. "We've both been fired!"

Amelia Bedelia was amazed to learn that being let go was the same as being fired. It reminded her that she still had to go home and tell her parents what had happened at Pete's. She got up to leave.

"Hey, Diana, maybe you should start your own business," she said.

Diana nodded. "I think you're right," she said. "I'd never fire myself. I would be fireproof."

"If you were fireproof," said Amelia Bedelia, "you'd never get burned."

"Right you are!" said Diana.

Amelia Bedelia scratched Buster behind his ears and said good-bye to Diana. But she didn't get very far.

"Excuse me, miss! Excuse me!" A man was waving at her.

"Miss," he said, "I'm meeting someone here for the first time—well, it's a date— and I told her I'd be carrying a bouquet. Would you please sell me yours?"

"It's for my mom," said Amelia Bedelia.

"I'll pay you ten dollars!" he said.

Amelia Bedelia shook her head. "No, I promised."

"How about twenty dollars?" he asked.

Twenty dollars!

"Here you go," she said, handing him the bouquet of flowers.

"Thanks!" he said, handing her a crisp twenty-dollar bill.

Twenty dollars! Amelia Bedelia waved to Diana and was on her way once again. But then she heard a familiar voice. She peeked over her shoulder.

The policeman had stopped the man with the bouquet.

Amelia Bedelia began to walk faster.

"Excuse me, sir," said the policeman. "Those flowers look suspiciously like the ones we grow in the park. Where did you get them?"

"I just bought them," she heard the man answer. "From a sweet little girl."

Amelia Bedelia began to trot.

"What little girl?" asked the policeman.

Amelia Bedelia began to run. She darted through the park gates, running as fast as she could. She flew by a sign that said SLOW CHILDREN. *I'm not having much luck with signs today,* she thought as she raced home.

By the time she got to her house, Amelia Bedelia was out of breath. Her parents did not seem surprised to see her.

"We got a call from Pete," said Amelia Bedelia's father. "Next time, call us and we'll come get you."

"There won't be a next time," said Amelia Bedelia.

"Oh, sweetie," her mom said. "It was a good try."

"What did you learn from your first job?" asked her father.

"I learned that the customer is always right," said Amelia Bedelia.

"That's what they say," said her father.

"Did you learn anything else?" asked her mother.

"Yes," said Amelia Bedelia. "I learned that sometimes the customer is crazy!"

Amelia Bedelia's parents smiled. They stopped when they saw Amelia Bedelia's lower lip begin to tremble.

"It's no fun to get fired," sobbed Amelia Bedelia. "Now I'll never get that bike!"

Her parents hugged her and hoisted her up into their arms. "Don't worry," they said. "We have an idea."

Chapter 7

The Lemonade S~~tand~~ sit

"You know," said Amelia Bedelia's father, "your mom and I think you should start your own business. And there is one business that *any* kid can start."

"What?" said Amelia Bedelia.

"A lemonade stand," said her dad.

"Lemonade what?" said Amelia Bedelia.

"Stand," said her dad.

"Stand?" she said. "Stand what?"

"Lemonade," said her dad.

"Sure," said Amelia Bedelia. "I can stand lemonade. I love lemonade."

Her father rolled his eyes and said, "I know you love lemonade, sweetie. That's why you should make a stand for it."

"How come?" said Amelia Bedelia. "Is someone trying to get rid of lemonade?"

Amelia Bedelia's dad's face began to turn red. "Of course not," he said. "You could run a stand."

Amelia Bedelia looked bewildered.

"Dad," she asked, "what do you want me to do—run or stand?"

"Stand!" yelled her dad. "Stand! Stand!" Amelia Bedelia jumped to her feet.

"Okay, okay!" she said. "I'm standing, I'm standing!"

Now her dad's face was turning even redder.

"No," he said. "Not you. Your customers stand. You can sit."

"Thank you," said Amelia Bedelia. She sat back down in her chair.

"Good idea," said her dad. "I think I need to sit down, too."

Amelia Bedelia's mother had been in the kitchen, listening to them talk while she finished up. She was carrying a cup of coffee as she came into the living room. She sat down on the arm of her husband's chair.

"Amelia Bedelia," she said, "remember last summer? We made fresh lemonade together."

"It was delicious," said Amelia Bedelia.

"And easy," said her mother. "Do you remember how we made it?"

"You squeeze juice out of a lemon, mix it with cool water, add sugar until it tastes good, then throw in a couple of ice cubes."

"Bravo," said her mother. "Then what?"

Amelia Bedelia shrugged and said, "That's easy. You drink it!"

"Or," said her mother, "you could sell it. What if you set up a table and made fresh lemonade? Thirsty people would stand in line to drink it."

"You know," said Amelia Bedelia, "that sort of sounds like what Dad was trying to say."

"Thank you," said Amelia Bedelia's father. Then he turned to his wife and said,

"And thank you, darling. I couldn't have said it better myself."

Amelia Bedelia bought fifty bags of lemons on sale. She used the money she'd saved from her last birthday, her tip from Pete's Diner, plus the twenty dollars she got for her bouquet. Her dad helped her build a stand that was easy to set up and take down.

"That way," he said, "you can put it up wherever you'll get the most customers."

"Have you thought of a name for yourself?" asked her mom.

"My name is Amelia Bedelia," she said. "That's the name you guys gave me."

"I meant," said her mom, "a name for your business—something catchy to get people's attention."

"Yes," said her dad. "Think big."

"How can I?" said Amelia Bedelia. "My brain is just one size."

"Maybe you should advertise," said her mom. "If people hear how good your lemonade is, they'll want to try it."

"Advertise?" said Amelia Bedelia.

"Like the commercials on TV for Wild Bill's Auto-Rama?"

"Sort of," said her dad. "But not so terrible."

Everybody knew about Wild Bill's Auto-Rama. Bill owned a car dealership right downtown. He wore a white ten-gallon cowboy hat. In his TV ads, he shouted over and over and over that to get the best price, you had to buy your new car from Wild Bill's Auto-Rama, the Home of the Sweet Deal.

Suddenly Amelia Bedelia had a great idea. She remembered last summer, when her parents had dragged her along to Wild Bill's to look at new cars with them. It was boring and hot—she could really have used a break. If she set up her stand near Wild Bill's Auto-Rama, plenty of thirsty customers would line up for her lemonade when they were tired of looking at cars.

Amelia Bedelia hopped on her awful, embarrassing, piece-of-junk bike and rode down to Wild Bill's Auto-Rama. She found the ideal spot for her stand, right near the entrance. Perfect! This was meant to be. She pedaled home as fast as she could. As she turned into her driveway, a great name for her business popped into her head.

Hooray!

"Mom!" yelled Amelia Bedelia. "Do you have

any yellow paint left over from when you painted the kitchen? I need to make my sign."

"Sure, sweetie," said her mom. She also gave Amelia Bedelia brushes and an old bedsheet.

Amelia Bedelia spread the sheet out on the driveway and went to work. Her dad had told her to think big. So she drew a lemon as large as the kitchen table and outlined it with black marker. She was in the middle of writing the name for her business right on top of the lemon when her mom and dad came out to peek at what she was doing.

"Mom! Dad! Stop!" hollered Amelia Bedelia.

"Don't look—I want you to be surprised!"

They certainly were. So was Wild Bill. And so were the reporters from the TV Action News Team, as well as everyone in town.

Chapter 8

Amelia Bedelia's Last Stand

The next day, Amelia Bedelia waited until just before lunchtime to open for business. She figured that by then, people would be hot and thirsty and bored enough to want a glass of lemonade.

Her parents came along to help. Her dad set up her lemonade stand while her mom unfolded the sign. They attached it

to the bottom of the sign for Wild Bill's
Auto-Rama.

"Looking good," said her dad.

"Terrific name," said her mom.

"It's perfect," said Amelia Bedelia. "I
squeeze a whole lemon into every glass.
That's a lot."

Amelia Bedelia was so proud of her sign.

She admired it
while her dad set
up chairs in front of the stand.

"Thanks, Daddy," said Amelia Bedelia. "Now my customers won't have to stand. This is more like a lemonade sit than a stand."

Her father kept checking his watch. "I have a surprise for you," he said. "I called the television station and told them about your business. They thought it was a cute idea. They're sending their news team to interview you."

Amelia Bedelia jumped up and clapped her hands. "Really? Will they make a commercial for me?"

"Nope," said her dad. "You'll be a story

on *News at Noon*. That's way better than a commercial. It's the real deal."

"Dad and I are going inside to look at the cars for a few minutes," said her mom. "We'll send some customers out here for you."

"Thanks," said Amelia Bedelia. "I'll get ready." She cut lemons in half and put them in a big bowl ready to squeeze. Then she arranged the cups and ice.

A few minutes later, a van from the Action News Team pulled up. They were her first customers. A reporter and a cameraman walked up to the stand and introduced themselves to Amelia Bedelia. As she talked with them about her business, she made them each a lemonade.

The cameraman started shooting the scene, while the reporter began interviewing Amelia Bedelia.

To truly appreciate what happened next, you'd have to have seen it on TV. Down at Pete's Diner, Pete and Doris always turned on *News at Noon* for their lunch crowd. Here is what they saw:

"Ted Daily here, *News at Noon*, right outside Wild Bill's Auto-Rama, where another business is having its grand opening: an old-fashioned lemonade stand run by this young lady—"

"It's Amelia Bedelia!" said Pete. A policeman who was having pie and coffee at the counter looked up and said,

"You know her, Pete? I had a run-in with that girl in the park."

Pete nodded and said, "Officer O'Brien, be glad Doris served you that cherry pie you're eating!"

They looked back at the TV. Ted Daily told the viewers how Amelia Bedelia made her lemonade while the cameraman shot a close-up.

"Amelia Bedelia makes every glass by hand . . . just lemon juice, cool water, ice, and a bit of sugar," Ted Daily said.

Amelia Bedelia handed Ted Daily a glass of lemonade. "I use one lemon in each glass," she said. "That's a lot, but it tastes better. It's why I call my business Lots of Lemons."

As Amelia Bedelia pointed at the sign behind her, the camera pulled back so people watching on television could also see the sign for Wild Bill's Auto-Rama.

"You folks at home take it from me, Ted Daily. Amelia Bedelia's lemonade may be a sweeter deal than you'll get at Wild Bill's Auto-Rama!"

Amelia Bedelia was thrilled! Her dad was right. Being on the news was great! Her lemonade was going to be famous, and maybe, just maybe,

she'd make enough money to buy half of a new bike.

That's when the camera began to jiggle up and down. The cameraman could not hold it steady because he was laughing so hard.

Back at the diner, Pete said, "Looks like an earthquake at Wild Bill's!"

Doris covered her mouth with her hand and gasped, "Gracious! Amelia Bedelia's sign makes Wild Bill's cars look like lemons."

Pete shut his eyes and shook his head.

Back at Wild Bill's, Ted Daily turned around to see what was so funny.

He looked at Amelia Bedelia's sign, too, and doubled over with laughter. Then Wild Bill himself came out to see what was going on. Amelia Bedelia was so impressed to see him in person. He was a real celebrity!

"Howdy, fellas," said Wild Bill. "What can I do for you? Are you in the market for a new car?"

Ted and his cameraman tried not to laugh, but that just made it worse.

"What's so funny there, fellas?" asked Wild Bill.

Ted pointed to Amelia Bedelia's sign. He was laughing so hard he could barely stand up.

"Lots of Lemons!" read Wild Bill.

"That's a sweet idea on a hot day like this." Then the joke dawned on Wild Bill, too.

"Lots of lemons?" he bellowed. *"Lots of lemons?* I don't sell lemons. My cars are the best! My cars are not lemons!"

"Of course not," said Amelia Bedelia. "Cars are cars. Lemons are lemons." She handed him a glass of her lemonade. "Here," she said. "My treat!"

"I'm not gonna stand for this!" he said.

"You don't have to," said Amelia Bedelia. "Have a seat. That's why I brought chairs with me."

Wild Bill bent down to look at Amelia Bedelia eye-to-eye. "Little lady," he said, "are you mockin' me with your lemonade?"

"Oh, no, sir, you're famous," said Amelia Bedelia. She pointed at the TV camera. "Everyone knows you."

Wild Bill looked straight into the camera. "Is that thing on?" he asked. His face turned from white as a ghost to red to white again. He strode toward the camera, took off his cowboy hat, and used all ten gallons of it to cover the camera lens. Television screens all over town went dark.

Back at the diner, Doris and Pete and the policeman stared up at the blank screen. "Be glad you're not Amelia Bedelia right now," Doris whispered to Pete.

Chapter 9

If Life Hands You Lemons . . . Oh, Never Mind

Like Diana's pink slip, the aftermath of Amelia Bedelia's lemonade stand fiasco was not at all pretty. Amelia Bedelia to̶k̶ ̶c̶over in the car showroom until the gr̶u̶w̶n̶̶s̶ps sorted things out.

The TV station agreed to run Wild Bill's commercials for the next three months for free. Amelia Bedelia's parents agreed that she would not sell any more lemonade for thirty days, and then—if she still wanted to run her lemonade business—she would stay a mile away from Wild Bill's.

Back home, Amelia Bedelia faced a new worry. "What am I going to do with fifty bags of lemons?" she moaned. "I've got five hundred lemons!"

"Well, you know what they say," her dad said. "If life hands you lemons, you make . . . uh, you make . . ." His voice trailed off. He stopped before he said that dreaded word, "lemonade."

"You make what?" asked Amelia Bedelia. "What do you make?"

"You make the best of it," said her mom.

Amelia Bedelia's dad looked very relieved, for some reason. Her mom continued, "You can make lemon squares, lemon marmalade, lemon tarts. . . ."

"Oh, Mom, lemons are tart to begin with," said Amelia Bedelia. "They're born tart."

"Yes," said her mom. "That's why a lemon tart is so tasty. You know what? I'm craving lemon tarts right this minute. Let's make a big batch!"

Amelia Bedelia and her mother headed for the kitchen. Amelia Bedelia's mother gathered the ingredients, got out her tart pans, and showed Amelia Bedelia how to make lemon tarts. Amelia Bedelia added extra lemons to the recipe—she had tons to use up, after all!

Amelia Bedelia and her mother and father each ate a slice of lemon tart as soon as they had cooled. As her dad savored his last bite, he squeezed his eyes shut and shivered. "Wow," he said, "that was one *tart* tart!"

Bingo! Amelia Bedelia knew exactly how she would use up all of her lemons. She would make lemon tarts for everyone she knew, adding extras lemon to make them extra tart and extra special!

The next day, Amelia Bedelia got right to work. She discovered a small tart pan in the pantry. It was perfect. With just a little bit of help from her mom, she baked a dozen bite-sized tarts. She packed them carefully in her lunch box and put that in the basket of her miserable, rusty,

beat-up bike. Then she headed off to Pete's Diner.

As she took a shortcut through the park, Amelia Bedelia saw the pink-slip lady sitting on the same bench as before.

Only now, instead of having just one dog, she was surrounded by at least a dozen dogs of all shapes and sizes and colors.

"Hello, Pink-Slip Lady," Amelia Bedelia called out as she rode up.

"That's me!" said Diana, laughing. "And you must be that famous lemonade lady I saw on television, right?"

Amelia Bedelia parked her bike next to Diana and the dogs.

"Guess what? I took your advice," said Diana. "I started my own business, too. Here it is." She opened her arms to the dogs.

"I loved walking my own dog so much that I decided to do it for a living. Now I'm a professional dog walker and trainer. See how well behaved they are?"

"Wow," said Amelia Bedelia. "Can they do tricks?"

"Sure," said Diana. "But usually I need treats to inspire them, and I'm all out. I'll have to pack more tomorrow."

"Do they like the taste of lemons?" asked Amelia Bedelia. She took out her lunch box and gave Diana a tart to taste.

"Amazing," said Diana. "It's so little and yet so tart!"

"I make a very tart tart," said Amelia Bedelia. "Do you think the dogs would like them?"

Diana broke off a piece of lemony tart and put it on top of Buster's wet nose. He didn't move. He just sat there

 with the tiny piece balanced on his nose. "He doesn't like it," said Amelia Bedelia.

"No," said Diana. "I've trained him well. Watch this." Diana snapped her fingers. Buster sat up, flipped the piece of tart into the air, opened his mouth, and gulped it right down. He wagged his tail happily.

"He does like it," said Amelia Bedelia. She looked over at the other dogs. They were looking at Buster and at Amelia Bedelia, then at Buster, then back at her. "What about them? Can they try a tart, too?"

"How many do you have?" said Diana.

Amelia Bedelia set aside enough tarts for Pete and Doris. Then Diana showed her how to make the dogs sit and lie down and roll over and jump into the air. When the tarts were all gone, the dogs gazed at Amelia Bedelia and wagged their tails wildly.

"Look at them," said Diana. "You made lots of furry friends today. They'll never forget your tarts or you."

"Thanks, Diana," said Amelia Bedelia. "I love dogs." She patted them all one last time, got back on her bike, and waved as she rode away.

"Hey, Amelia Bedelia!" Diana called. "You should start a new business. You could call it Tart Tarts!"

Amelia Bedelia tried to ring the bell on her handlebars to let Diana know that she loved her suggestion, but it was broken and didn't make a sound.

On her way to Pete's Diner, Amelia Bedelia took a detour by Wild Bill's Auto-Rama. He wasn't there, so she left a tart for him with a note. She wrote:

I'm sorry again about the sign. Here is one lemon I hope you'll like.

Yours truly,

Amelia Bedelia

Chapter 10

Cheaper by the ½ Dozen

When Amelia Bedelia walked into Pete's Diner, people turned to look at her.

I'm embarrassed, she thought. *I hope they weren't here when I stepped on that piece of pie.* Then she heard whispering.

"That's her!"

"Her? Are you sure?"

"Sure I'm sure."

"It's that little lemonade lady."

Amelia Bedelia began to blush. She was so happy to finally see Doris. Doris gave her a huge hug.

"Hi, Amelia Bedelia!" she said. "We saw you on TV. You're a big star now!"

Amelia Bedelia was still blushing and had started to explain what had really happened when Pete came out of the kitchen.

"Look who's here," he said. "Step on any pies lately? Or did you come back here to kick our coconut cake?"

Amelia Bedelia sat on a stool at the counter. "I came to apologize," she said. "You gave me my first job, but I didn't do a very good job at it."

Pete took a plate of hot french fries

from a passing waiter and set it down in front of her.

"Oh, yummy!" said Amelia Bedelia. "But I don't have enough money to . . ."

"Relax," said Pete. "It's on the house."

"Whose house?" she asked. "On your house?"

"Never mind," he said. "They're on the counter and they're on me . . . I mean, they're free."

"Thanks!" said Amelia Bedelia. She put her lunch box next to the plate of fries and dug in.

"What's that for?" asked Pete. "Did you bring your own lunch?"

"No," said Amelia Bedelia. "I have a present for you and Doris." She opened her lunch box and took out her last two lemon tarts.

Pete took one look at the tarts and declared, "Time for a coffee break!" He poured two cups of coffee while Doris put the tarts on plates and got two forks.

"Wow! They look terrific," said Doris.

"They taste even better," said Pete.

"Do you really like them?" asked Amelia Bedelia. "You bake such delicious brownies—they're famous!"

"Hah!" said Pete. "A great lemon tart takes a lot of skill. My brownies are a dime a dozen."

"A dime for a dozen?" said Amelia Bedelia. "That's a good deal!" She dug deep down in her pocket, pulled out a nickel,

12 for 10 cents = good deal

and put it on the
counter. "I'll take
six brownies, to go."
Doris chuckled.
"Coming right up,
hon," she said.
"You're a better
businessman than Pete!"

"Keep your money, Amelia Bedelia,"
said Pete. "Just bring me two dozen of
your little lemon tart tarts every day. I'll
pay you fifty cents apiece."

Doris did the math quickly in her head.
"That's twelve dollars a day!" she said.
"Do you think you can do it?"

Amelia Bedelia thought it over for at least half a second. Then she gave Doris a thumbs-up and Pete her firmest handshake ever. "You've got a deal!"

Amelia Bedelia headed for home. She felt great. And she had baking to do! She cut through the park, pedaling as fast as she could. She sped up when she saw the policeman. Then she flew past Diana

and the dogs. The dogs began to bark and pull at their leashes. Amelia Bedelia looked over her shoulder and waved at them. That was when she ran into Suzanne Scroggins. Literally.

Both girls were thrown off their bikes. Both bikes crashed to the ground. Amelia Bedelia rolled across the grass and came to a stop at the edge of the flower bed. Suzanne skidded down the sidewalk.

Amelia Bedelia dusted herself off, then went to see if Suzanne was okay.

"Are you all right?" asked Amelia Bedelia.

"I guess so," said Suzanne. She pointed at Amelia Bedelia's elbow. "You're bleeding."

Amelia Bedelia pointed at Suzanne's knee. "So are you."

"Why did you run into me?" Suzanne demanded. "Are you trying to wreck my bike?"

"What do you mean?" asked Amelia Bedelia. "It was an accident."

Amelia Bedelia remembered that Doris had tucked a napkin into the box of brownies. "Here." She gave the napkin to Suzanne. "Wipe your knee."

Suzanne looked in the box and said, "*Ewwww*, gross. What's that?"

"They used to be six brownies from Pete's Diner," Amelia Bedelia said, laughing. "I must have landed on them when we crashed. They got smushed into one big chocolate pancake."

Suzanne smiled. "That's a good thing. It looks like they broke your fall."

Amelia Bedelia tore off a piece of the big brownie and ate it. "They still taste great. I'd love to have this pancake for breakfast. Here, try some, Suzanne."

She gave her a piece.

"Call me Suzi," said Suzanne. "Wow—this is yummy!"

Suzanne said goodbye to Amelia Bedelia and got back on her bike. But when she tried to pedal away, the wheel made a scraping sound.

"Uh-oh," said Amelia Bedelia.

"No problem," said Suzanne. "The bike shop where we got it is right by the park entrance. Do you want to come with me and see if they can fix it?"

Amelia Bedelia and Suzanne walked their bikes over to the bike shop. It was called The Spokes People. While the owner of the shop, whose name was Marcus Smith, repaired the wheel, they wandered among the rows of bikes for sale. Above her, hanging from the ceiling, Amelia Bedelia saw a beautiful bike. It was just like Suzanne's, but it was red. "One day, that will be my bike," she vowed.

"If either of you ladies wants to get a new bike," Marcus said, "here is your chance." He tapped a poster on the wall behind him. It read:

ANNUAL DOWNTOWN
CELEBRATION AND BIKE PARADE!
FIRST PRIZE: THE BIKE OF YOUR DREAMS!

"Listen to this," said Suzanne as she read the poster. "'Decorate your bike for the parade. This year's theme is individuality. The winner can select the bike of her dreams from The Spokes People.'"

Amelia Bedelia was excited but wary. So far, signs had given her nothing but problems. Maybe this poster would change her luck. She did have one question. "What kind of decorations can we put on our bikes?"

Marcus shrugged. "Good question," he said. "Since the theme is individuality, I guess you can do whatever you want. If I were you, I'd use plenty of imagination and be as original as you can."

He spun the wheels on Suzanne's bike. They turned smoothly. "All done," said Marcus. "And it's on the house."

"Whose house?" asked Amelia Bedelia. "Your house or Pete's?"

"Huh?" Marcus asked.

"Thanks!" yelled Suzanne, as she and Amelia Bedelia rode off together.

"Good luck, ladies!" called Marcus.

Chapter 11

Dream Bike Nightmares

As she rode home, Amelia Bedelia got more and more excited about the contest. She told her mom and dad all about it.

"When I win," she said, "I'll get a free bike, and you won't have to pay for half."

"That's nice, honey," said her mom. "We'll add the money we would have given you to your college fund instead.

We're so proud of you. You're doing a great job trying to earn your half!"

In her excitement, Amelia Bedelia had forgotten all about baking tarts for Pete's.

"Hey, I got a job!" she announced. "Pete liked my tarts so much that he wants me to bake two dozen a day. He'll sell them at the diner."

"Congratulations!" said her mom. "Lots of people go to Pete's. Did you know that the mayor eats at the diner every day? If he likes your tarts, your business could be a big hit. The best advertising is by word of mouth."

"Mom's right," said Amelia Bedelia's father.

"You know, winning a contest is a long shot."

"Dad, I'm decorating a bike," said Amelia Bedelia. "Not playing basketball."

"Hey," said her dad, "I have an idea. Why don't you decorate your bike like a giant lemon tart? You'll attract more customers and make more money. Then you can buy your bike. That's a sure thing."

"You sure that's sure?" said Amelia Bedelia. She turned to her mom. "What do you think?"

"That's a tough one," said her mother. "I can see Dad's point of view. But I also see that you want to try and win the contest." Amelia Bedelia's mother smiled. "That means there's only one way to settle this.

Get ready, you two."

She took a quarter out of her purse and flipped it high in the air.

"Tails!" shouted Amelia Bedelia.

"Heads!" called out Amelia Bedelia's dad.

Heads it was.

So Amelia Bedelia took her dad's advice. She worked on her bike right up to the morning of the parade.

Both sides of the front wheel looked like giant lemon slices. Both sides of the back wheel looked like giant lemon tarts.

On her back, Amelia Bedelia wore a sign that looked like a mouthwatering slice of tart. On the slice she had written, TRY A BITE! Next to the word "bite," she had cut out a big toothy bite. It was a great white shark–size bite.

To top it all off, Amelia Bedelia constructed a papier-mâché lemon to cover her helmet. She had painted it yellow. It even had a stem and bright green leaves that fluttered in the breeze.

"If I were you," said her dad, "I would take along some lemon tarts and hand them out to people as samples. That way you can peddle your tarts all over town."

Her dad chuckled to himself. Amelia Bedelia guessed that he must have made some kind of joke about being on a bike and selling tarts. She didn't have time to figure it out. And from the way her mom was shaking her head and rolling her eyes, it surely wasn't worth understanding, anyway.

Chapter 12

"Try a Bite!"—NOT!

Amelia Bedelia rode her bike to the town square, where the parade was assembling. Suzanne was already there. When Amelia Bedelia saw Suzanne's bike, she was speechless. She felt exactly the way she felt the very first time she saw T.H.E. BIKE.

Suzanne had woven red, orange,

yellow, green, blue, and violet crepe paper into the spokes of her wheels. When they went around, the colors revolved in a spiral into the center of the wheel. It looked like a swirling rainbow. Suzanne had glued glittery stars in the center of both wheels. Amelia Bedelia was so dizzy she had to look away! Was Suzanne trying to hypnotize the judges into voting for her? There were also rainbow-colored streamers flowing out of the ends of her handlebars, tiny flags, bunting made out of little paper unicorns, and jingle bells hanging everywhere.

On the bright side, Amelia Bedelia was glad that she had not wasted her time trying to

116

compete with Suzanne. Maybe Suzanne would toss her the not-new-anymore bike as she rode away on her *brand-new* bike.

The poster in the bike shop had not mentioned that there was a pet parade, too. Amelia Bedelia could see cats, rabbits, goldfish, guinea pigs, snakes, mice, and dogs, dogs, and more dogs!

Another thing the poster hadn't mentioned was that Wild Bill was the celebrity judge of the bike contest! He was riding with the mayor and Miss Individuality in one of his convertibles at the front of the parade. Now Amelia Bedelia was doubly glad that she hadn't tried to win—Wild Bill would never pick her in a million years.

 She peeked under the bright yellow dish towel in her bike basket. There were her lemon tarts, all ready to hand out to people in the crowd as she rode by.

Soon it was time for the parade to begin. The non-dog pets followed the convertible, then came the dogs, then the kids on their bikes. The crowd cheered and clapped for all of the marchers. When Amelia Bedelia pedaled past her parents, they clapped loudest of all. "Hooray for Tart Tarts!" her dad yelled.

Amelia Bedelia waved, blushed, and pretended not to know them.

Then it started. Maybe it was triggered

by her dad yelling "tart tarts"! As Amelia Bedelia pedaled by one of the dogs, it turned and looked straight at her. It put its nose in the air and sniffed. Then it began to wag its tail and bark. And bark. And BARK!

Amelia Bedelia recognized that dog. It was one of the dogs Diana had been walking. And it had loved the taste of her lemon tarts.

Suddenly a dog on the other side of the street started barking. *Uh-oh.* It had tasted her tarts, too. As Amelia Bedelia rode on, dogs started sniffing, wagging, barking, and straining at their leashes, trying to get as close as possible to her.

Amelia Bedelia peeked in her bike

basket. No wonder these dogs were barking. The basket was filled with tasty tart tarts, and they smelled delicious. Amelia Bedelia decided then and there that this would be the perfect time to give out her tarts. If she passed them out now, maybe the dogs would leave her alone. She also decided that she would never listen to her father ever again. Pedaling tarts? Ha, ha! Very funny, Dad!

"Come back here, Bruno!"

Amelia Bedelia looked
behind her. Bruno had broken

Stop!

away and was running to catch up with her.

"Someone grab my dog!"

Another dog had broken away. Amelia Bedelia pedaled faster.

"Lucky! Stop! Stay!"

And another. And another.

"Hey, grab that leash!"

It seemed as though all the dogs in town were chasing Amelia Bedelia and her tart tarts. Maybe it was because they didn't want to miss out on a treat. Or maybe this was how dogs celebrated their spirit of individuality. Or maybe they just loved Amelia Bedelia.

She was weaving in and out of the other bicycles and marchers. She pedaled as fast as she could on her old bike,

121

with her lemon head bobbing wildly.

"Faster!" yelled Suzanne, who had seen what was happening. She rode behind Amelia Bedelia, swerving back and forth, trying to keep the dogs away. Several of Amelia Bedelia's friends from school pedaled up and tried to help, too.

"Go, Amelia Bedelia!" yelled Joy.

"Faster!" called Chip.

Tweet! Tweet! There was the policeman from the park. He blew his whistle at Amelia Bedelia and held up his hand to signal her to STOP! Amelia Bedelia glanced over her shoulder. She had never seen so many dogs! She reached into her basket, pulled out a tart, and put it in the policeman's hand as she sped by.

He blew his whistle even louder. She looked back and saw a dog leap through the air. It grabbed the tart right out of the policeman's hand, like a porpoise snatching a sardine from a sailor. The policeman stared at his hand and counted. "One, two, three, four, five!" All of his fingers were present and accounted for. "Whew!"

Amelia Bedelia saw Pete and Doris up ahead. She reached into her basket and handed them tarts as she pedaled by.

"Eat them quick or—" she warned.

Pete and Doris were too slow.

A pair of poodles leaped up and—GULP! GULP!—those tarts were history.

GULP! GULP!

Amelia Bedelia had almost reached the head of the parade. There were still dogs everywhere. She wasn't sure what to do, but she knew she had to get rid of her tarts! She rode in a loop-de-loop pattern. Then in a circle. Then she headed back the way she had come. Everyone was following her—dogs, their owners, and all of the kids on their decorated bikes. Amelia Bedelia handed out tarts left and right. Some folks actually got a taste!

As Amelia Bedelia rode past the convertible, she tossed her tarts to the celebrities. Miss Individuality caught hers with one slender white-gloved hand. The mayor used both hands. Wild Bill was waving his cowboy hat at the

crowd as though he
was riding a bronco
instead of riding in a
car. Amelia Bedelia
tossed her last tart
right into his hat. Bull's-eye!

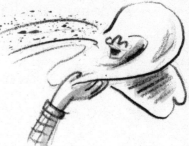

Amelia Bedelia had run out of tarts just
as she had run out of parade. But the dogs
were still chasing her. The air was full of
their barking. Then it dawned on Amelia
Bedelia that her bike looked like a huge dog
treat. Even worse, the words "Try a Bite!"
were printed on her back. These dogs
were pretty smart. Could any of them
read? Amelia Bedelia promised herself
that if she survived today, she'd never have
anything to do with signs again.

Amelia Bedelia had to keep moving. She circled around and pulled up behind Wild Bill's convertible. She jumped off her bike and let it clatter to the ground. Miss Individuality helped her climb into the backseat of the car. Amelia Bedelia ripped the enormous tart off her shirt and threw it to the dogs. They had a blast tearing it apart, howling with happiness all the while.

Amelia Bedelia slid down onto the seat next to Wild Bill. He took one look at the giant lemon bobbing on her head and said, "Not you again!"

Woof! Woof! Woof! The dogs were barking and drooling and circling the convertible.

Woof! Woof! Woof!

"Get us out of Dodge!" yelled Wild Bill to the driver.

The driver put the car in reverse and backed up.

Kaaaaa-RUUNCH!

The screeching of metal being dragged across pavement brought the entire parade to a halt.

"What was that?" asked Wild Bill.

"That," said Amelia Bedelia, her eyes brimming with tears, "was my bike."

Chapter 13

So Who Needs Fireworks?

If you've ever wondered what utter chaos and confusion, mass mayhem, and perfect pandemonium would look like—well, this was it. Barking dogs darted back and forth, and kids on bikes swerved around one another and around pets of all shapes and sizes. The crowd clapped and cheered, cars honked their horns, the policeman blew his whistle . . . all, you might say, in the spirit of individuality.

The mayor managed to make his way to the grandstand. This was where, on every special occasion, he had given a speech to his calm, quiet, peaceful town.

Diana bounded up the stairs onto the grandstand. "Excuse me, Mr. Mayor," she called out as she rushed to the microphone. She blew her whistle with all her might, but mysteriously, there was no sound.

All of a sudden, every dog in town froze. Their ears went straight up, and they all turned to look at her. Then they put their tails between their legs, and every single one of them slowly slunk back to its owner.

The car horns stopped honking. The guinea pigs and rabbits and parrots stopped chattering. The kids on their bikes settled down. Everyone was quiet except for the policeman.

He kept blowing his whistle over and over again until the mayor tapped on the microphone, then said, "Officer O'Brien? *Shhhhhhhhhhh.*"

Shhhhh!!

At last, a perfect silence descended upon the entire town. Everyone moved closer to the grandstand to hear what the mayor had to say.

The mayor cleared his throat. "I'm not sure what happened here today," he said. "But it looks like one person is responsible. Would Amelia Bedelia please come up here?"

When Amelia Bedelia heard the mayor say her name, she wanted to climb into the glove compartment and curl up into a little ball. But she didn't. Wild Bill opened the car door for her and walked beside her to the grandstand.

"If it's any consolation," he whispered gruffly as they walked along, "I think you make one mean lemon tart, little lady."

"I didn't make it to be mean," said Amelia Bedelia. "I made it to apologize."

"Apology accepted," said Wild Bill.

Amelia Bedelia wasn't sure what to do. Her tarts had caused this. She was to blame. What if the mayor made her pay to clean up the mess? Because there certainly was a big mess. Then she would never have enough money to get a new bike. And now she couldn't even jump on her old bike and escape. Her bike, her first sweet, wonderful, one-and-only bike was flatter than a chocolate brownie pancake.

She was too tired to escape, anyway. Besides, it's tough to blend in with a giant lemon stuck on your head. Her parents met her at the steps to the grandstand. Her dad gave her a thumbs-up. Her mom took off the big lemon helmet. Amelia Bedelia trudged up the stairs to meet the mayor and her doom.

The mayor shook her parents' hands. Then he brought Amelia Bedelia forward to stand next to him at the microphone.

"I was born and raised here," he said.

"So I can safely say that this town has seen more excitement in the past fifteen minutes than it has in the past fifty years. As your mayor, I want to say that that is a good thing. When it comes to excitement, Amelia Bedelia means business!"

People in the crowd began to nod their heads in agreement. Amelia Bedelia could hear kids from school screaming and hollering and whistling. She could see Suzanne smiling and Joy and Holly and Clay laughing and smiling together. Everyone knew that they would talk about this day for years to come.

Then Wild Bill stepped forward to the microphone, his hat in his hand. "Mr. Mayor, everyone in town knows that

I've had my differences with this little lady. However, I've come to admire her spirit. She does things her own way. If something goes wrong, she bounces back and tries again. As far as I'm concerned, no one captures the spirit of individuality better than Amelia Bedelia. I declare her to be the winner of the bicycle contest!" As the crowd cheered, Wild Bill bent down to say to her, "I believe you could use a new bike. Am I right?"

Amelia Bedelia nodded and smiled and waved to the crowd. As the clapping died down, Wild Bill reached into his hat and pulled out the lemon tart Amelia Bedelia had tossed in. "And best of all," he said, "everyone in town should know that Amelia Bedelia makes one tasty lemon tart!" Wild Bill popped the tart into his mouth and wolfed it down in one bite. The crowd roared its approval again.

Amelia Bedelia looked over at her mom and dad and could only mouth the word "Thanks" because of all the cheering.

Chapter 14

The Bike Wheel of Fate Turns

On her first day back at school, Amelia Bedelia proudly locked her new bike to the bike rack. It was the same exact model as Suzanne's bike, but it was ruby red instead of emerald green. Amelia Bedelia loved it.

Suzanne rode up to the bike rack. But something was different. She wasn't smiling the way she had been after the parade. Then Amelia Bedelia got a good look at her bike. It was a wreck. It was in worse shape than Amelia Bedelia's old bike after it had been run over by the convertible.

Suzanne parked right next to Amelia Bedelia.

"What happened, Suzi?" asked Amelia Bedelia.

"I left my bike in the driveway," she said. "My mom didn't see it when she went to work, and she drove right over it. Her car got dinged up, too. I've never seen her that mad. She was jumping up and down and dancing around in the driveway!"

Amelia Bedelia tried not to laugh.

"It's not funny," said Suzanne. "My mom told me that I'm going to have to help pay for the damages. She said she would meet me halfway, though."

"I've been there," said Amelia Bedelia. "And I can tell you all about getting a job. Hey! I need someone to deliver my tarts.

I'll lend you my bike, and pay you."

Suzanne smiled. At first it was just a tiny smile, but then it grew bigger and bigger. Amelia Bedelia put her arm around Suzanne's shoulder, and she smiled, too. Then they walked into school together.

Amelia Bedelia

Unleashed

Hi!
Turn the page
for a special
sneak peek
at my next
adventure!

Read all these great books
about Amelia Bedelia!

#1

#2

#3

Coming soon!

Chapter 1

The Big Question

It certainly seemed like it was going to be another normal evening at Amelia Bedelia's house. Amelia Bedelia's mother was whirling around the kitchen, stirring, boiling, steaming, broiling, and tasting. Supper was almost ready. Something, however, was amiss.

For one thing, Amelia Bedelia's father

was sound asleep in his favorite chair. He was usually a big help in the kitchen. But he had looked so tired after work that Amelia Bedelia's mother had suggested that he take a little nap. For another thing, the dining room table wasn't set.

"Amelia Bedelia," said her mother, "have you set the table yet?"

Amelia Bedelia glanced up from her homework with a look that said, *Whoops! I forgot!* Then she jumped up to get the silverware.

"Remember the napkins!" her mother called.

"I do!" yelled Amelia Bedelia. "They're dark blue with little white flowers!"

"That's right," her mother said. "Please

remember to put them out for us."

"I'll do that now," said Amelia Bedelia.

"Thanks, sweetie," said her mother. "Do we need glasses?"

"Not yet," said Amelia Bedelia. "Only Dad wears them."

"Right again," said her mother. "I'll get you some water glasses to put out on the table."

"Oh," said Amelia Bedelia. "I already got those glasses."

"Did you fill them?" asked her mother.

"I sure did," said Amelia Bedelia.

Amelia Bedelia's mother peeked at the dining room table. Amelia Bedelia always did just what she was told to do, so every glass was filled right to the brim. Amelia

Bedelia's mother smiled and shook her head.

"Good job, sweetie," she said. "Now please take about a tablespoon of water out of each glass. Otherwise, we'll spill and make a mess."

"Okay," said Amelia Bedelia. She spooned some water out of her parents' glasses. Then she put her lips on the edge of her glass and . . .

SLURP!

"What's that noise?" called Amelia Bedelia's mother.

"That was me," said Amelia Bedelia. "Who did you think it was?"

"If I didn't know better," said her mother, "I could have sworn it was a

148

SLURP!!

SLURP!!

dog drinking out of a bowl."

"I'm glad you didn't swear," said Amelia Bedelia. "You always tell me not to swear. And I'm not a dog."

Two Ways to Say It

By Amelia Bedelia

"I'll meet you halfway."   "Let's compromise."

"Can you cut the mustard?"   "Can you do it well?"

"Step on it!"   "I'm in a hurry!"

"That's a piece of cake!"   "It's simple!"

"It costs an arm and a leg."   "That's expensive."

"Throw me a line!"   "Please help!"

"He is shorthanded."   "He doesn't have enough people to help him."